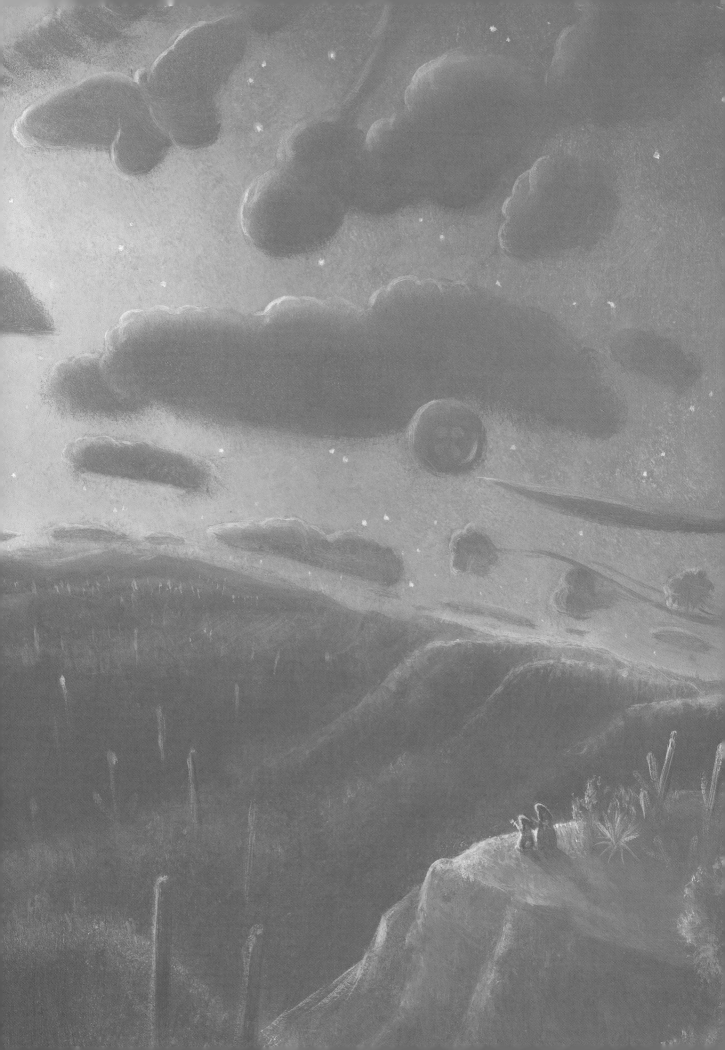

Remembering Grandpa

Uma Krishnaswami
Illustrated by Layne Johnson

BOYDS MILLS PRESS

HONESDALE, PENNSYLVANIA

For the real Daysha
        —U.K.

I first read this touching story . . . about one year after my own father passed away.
It touched me in such an honest way that I felt compelled to do the art for this book.
He and I did so many things together. Those happy moments will not be forgotten.
This book is dedicated to my parents.
        —L.J.

Boyds Mills Press, Inc.
A Highlights Company
815 Church Street
Honesdale, Pennsylvania 18431
Printed in China
www.boydsmillspress.com

Library of Congress Cataloging-in-Publication Data

Krishnaswami, Uma.
  Remembering Grandpa / Uma Krishnaswami ; illustrated by Layne Johnson.—1st ed.
    p. cm.
  Summary: When Grandma comes down with a "bad case of sadness"
one year after Grandpa's death, Daysha collects objects that will remind her
grandmother of Daysha's grandfather.
  ISBN-13: 978-1-59078-424-2 (hardcover : alk. paper)
  [1. Death—Fiction. 2. Sadness—Fiction. 3. Grandmothers—Fiction.
4. Grandfathers—Fiction. 5. Rabbits—Fiction.] I. Johnson, Layne, ill. II. Title.

PZ7.K8978Re 2007
  [E]—dc22

2006018273

First edition, 2007
The text of this book is set in 16-point Minion.
The illustrations are done in oils.

10 9 8 7 6 5 4 3 2 1

Daysha's grandpa
had been gone
for a year . . .

when her grandma
came down with
a bad case of sadness,
as if the turning of those
months without him
left a shadow in her life.

Sad wasn't how Daysha
remembered Grandpa,
so she set off to look for a cure.

Near the back step
where he used to sit
and play his guitar
and watch the sunrise,
she found a button that once
fell off Grandpa's old coat.
She put it in her wagon
and kept on looking.

Daysha climbed the hillside
where she and Grandpa
used to walk and talk
and chase the butterflies.
She gathered flowers and rocks
and added them
to the button in her wagon.

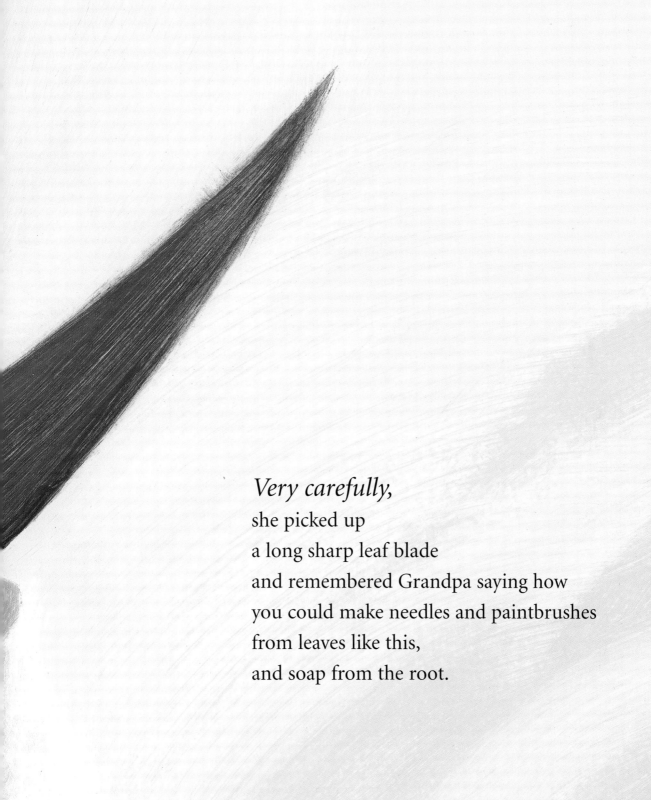

Very carefully,
she picked up
a long sharp leaf blade
and remembered Grandpa saying how
you could make needles and paintbrushes
from leaves like this,
and soap from the root.

Near an anthill,
Daysha found
a tiny chip of rock,
as blue as the stone
on Grandpa's belt buckle.

She found a
fine-scented branch
with fat berries on it . . .

a newly cast-off snakeskin,

wild bright flowers
on skinny stalks . . .

and black-and-white feathers
from a loud, proud bird.

Daysha went back home.
She made a pile of special things
in Grandpa's special sunrise place.

She strummed the strings
of Grandpa's old guitar
and laid it on the step,
feeling the little notes
rise up into the air.

Then she took Grandma's hand
and led her out to see
the special things she'd gathered
from places Grandpa loved.

"Oh, Daysha," said Grandma,
and she hugged her tightly.
Daysha cried a little,
and Grandma cried a lot,
and after she was done
she smiled and said . . .

"Thank you. That is the very nicest way
of remembering your grandpa
that anyone could think of."
Then Grandma took Daysha
for an ice cream,
just the way Daysha and Grandpa
went sometimes when he was well,
before the sad days.

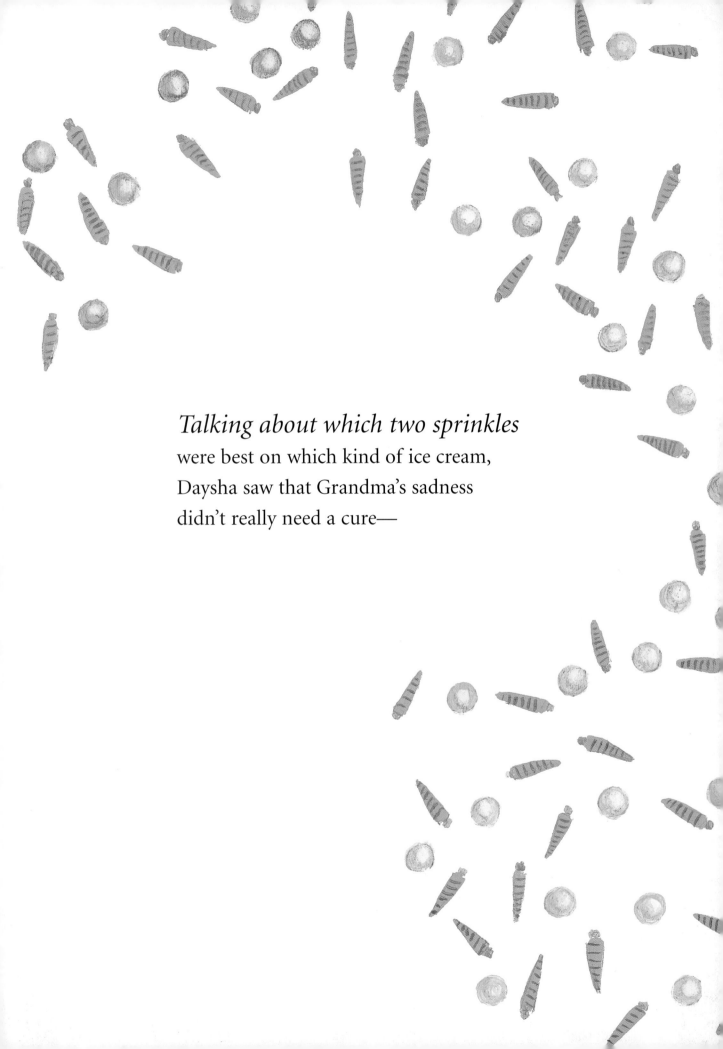

Talking about which two sprinkles
were best on which kind of ice cream,
Daysha saw that Grandma's sadness
didn't really need a cure—

just hugs,
and the right kind
of remembering.

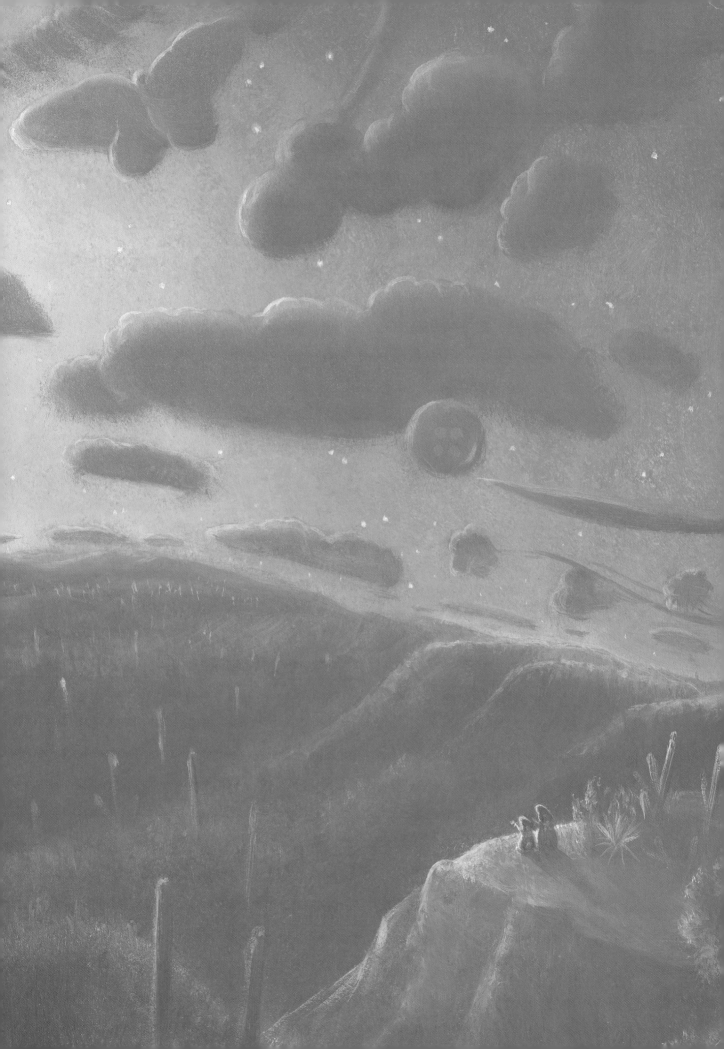

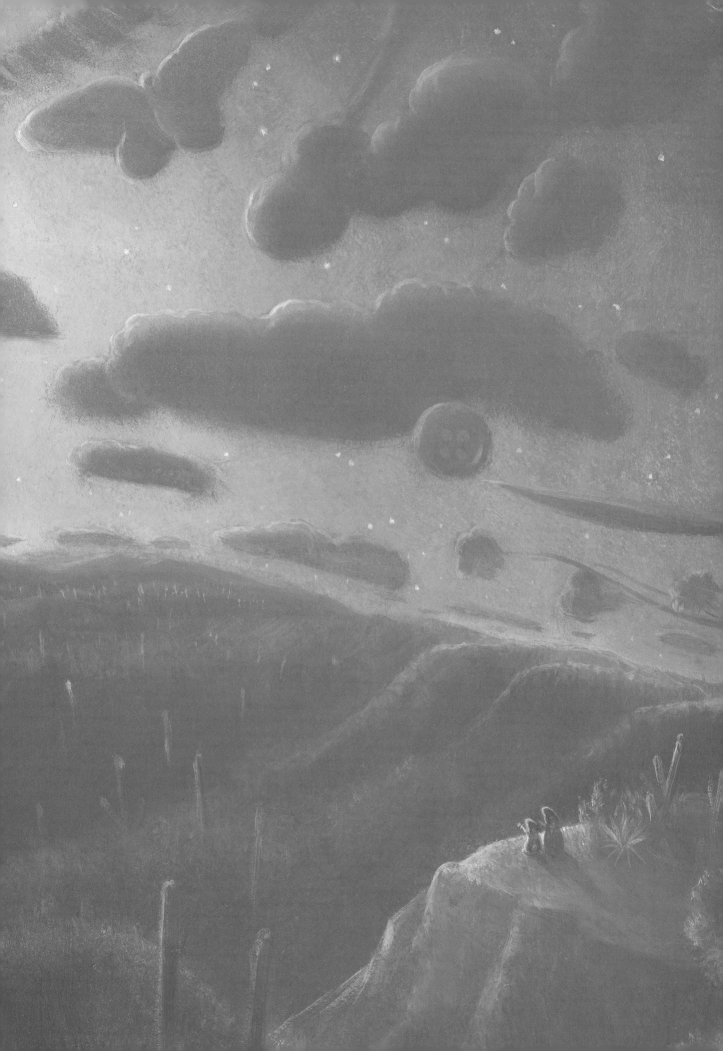